I Was There...

BOUDICA'S ARMY

While this book is based on real characters and actual historical events, some situations and people are fictional, created by the author.

Scholastic Children's Books
Euston House,
24 Eversholt Street
London, NW1 1DB, UK

A division of Scholastic Ltd
London ~ New York ~ Toronto ~ Sydney ~ Auckland
Mexico City ~ New Delhi ~ Hong Kong

First published in the UK by Scholastic Ltd, 2015

ISBN 978 1407 14884 7

Printed and bound by CPI Group (UK) Ltd, Croydon, CR0 4YY

1 3 5 7 9 10 8 6 4 2

I Was There...

BOUDICA'S ARMY

Hilary McKay

CHAPTER ONE

I am an Iceni girl. That's the name of our tribe, the British Iceni. We live in the wild, wide lands in the east of the country. We have lived in this land for always, I think. We were here long before the Romans. It's our land, not theirs, whatever they say.

My name is Kassy and I am ten years old. Finn, my brother, is three years older than me. My father is the man with the golden beard. He has golden hair too, but his head is shiny bare in the middle. He says that's my fault, for asking too many questions. Too many questions have made my father's hair slide off his head.

I live in a big round house in the middle
of our village with Finn and my father
and my Uncle Red and my grandmother.
Uncle Red and my father built the house
together and it is the biggest in the village.
Uncle Red and my father are the village
leaders, and our house is so big because it's
the place where people come when there
are arguments or sickness or other things
that need lots of talk. Uncle Red is good
at telling people what to do. My father is

good at making them laugh. Grandmother says Uncle Red used to be good at making people laugh too, but he gave it up when the Romans came.

Kassy means curly-haired. I was born with curly hair but now I just have tangles. I have tangles down to my shoulders and nobody can comb through them, not even my grandmother, and she can untangle almost anything. Spinning wool, arguments, the meaning of dreams. Honey from the honeycombs in the barley straw hives.

She can untangle the North Star from the star patterns in the sky, but she can't untangle my hair.

Finn's name has a meaning too. Finn means the fair one. But Finn is only fair when he is washed. Usually he is brown, brown-skinned and brown shaggy hair, just like his dog Brownie.

Finn and I have a grandmother to look after us instead of a mother. Our mother died long ago, when I was a baby. So then my grandmother had to start all over again.

Poor grandmother! She thought she had finished with wailing babies and wild wobbly little ones who scoop everything into their mouths and cannot be left with the fire. And as soon as we grew up from babies and little ones, we became the children who cause so much trouble. The ones who escape from the fieldwork to go swimming in the river, and creep from their beds at night time to visit the horses in the horse runs.

Finn and me.

I don't spin wool as quickly as I should and Finn whispered to me that he does not believe in any of the gods. We are not good children, my grandmother says. But my father says we're good enough for him.

"You are easily pleased!" said Uncle Red, but he winked at me when he said it.

I have a pony. I am the only girl in the village with a pony. I am the only girl my father has ever known with a pony. Perhaps I am the only Iceni girl in the country with a pony. Me! The only one.

"Do Roman girls have ponies?" I asked my father once.

"Not that I know of," said my father, and Uncle Red, who had heard, exclaimed, "Romans! Oily, murderous, stinking, lying, thousand-cursed thieves!"

"What, even the girls?" I asked, and Uncle Red said probably the girls were the worst of all. And before I could ask what was worse than all the things he had just said, he added, "And your father must have left his wits in the marsh to give a pony to a child like you!"

"Left my wits in the marsh!" roared my father, and he whacked Uncle Red on his shoulders as if he had made a good joke. "Uncle Red! A man of strong thoughts, eh Kassy?" he asked, laughing. "I think he is jealous because I have the only tangle-headed girl in the world with a honey-coloured pony of her own!"

I named my pony Honey when they gave her to me. It's the perfect name for her. Her coat is dark golden – honey coloured, and her mane and tail are beeswax fair. Her nose is bee-velvet soft.

She comes when I whistle, but not when anyone else whistles, not even Finn.

"She likes you best," said Finn one morning when we were out at the horse runs with Uncle Red. "It's not fair!"

"It is fair," I said. "Because all the other animals in the village like you best!"

Finn didn't say anything.

"It's true," I said. "They do. Even the pigs!"

"The pigs!" shouted Finn so wildly that even Uncle Red laughed at him. "Oh that's good! Oh that's wonderful! Am I to ride through the country on a pig then? Did you ever have a sister, Uncle Red?"

"The gods spared me that at least," said Uncle Red, and he took Finn away with him to help train the chariot ponies. They are bigger than Honey and every shade of shining brown, bright as autumn beech leaves, or as silver dark as oak. Just as pretty as Honey, but I like Honey best.

Honey is nearly three years old now, and as I am not very big or heavy, she is strong enough for me to ride. I do, like a boy, and my grandmother says it's shocking.

"Shocking!" she says often, but her eyes sparkle when she says it, not shocked at all, and she wove me a riding cloth of green and honey colour and stitched a little sheepskin on the back. She did that to make it soft for Honey when I strapped it on to ride.

"I think if you were a girl you would ride Honey too," I said to my grandmother once.

"Is that what you think?" she replied. "Well!"

"Well, what?" I asked.

"Perhaps I would," said my grandmother.

This is how Honey came to be mine.

Our village was famous for its horses.

Strong brave little horses with dark shining eyes and long tails to hit the flies away. Clever horses that can find a path in the dark and stand in quietness when you whisper, "Hush!"

But because our horses are clever they are also stubborn. They like to please us, but they like to please themselves too. Sometimes they don't want to work, and dance away from a halter, just out of reach. Sometimes they lean and lean and push and push on the fences that keep them safe from the marsh.

Sometimes, if we don't notice that the fence is no longer strong, they push right through.

That's what Honey's mother did when Honey was a tiny foal. She leaned against the fence until she pushed a gap and she got out through the gap and Honey followed after. That's how Honey got lost in the marsh.

The marsh! Our wide, flat eastern land, the Iceni land, is patched with marsh and bog. In places the earth holds so much water that the ground is like thin green porridge. You can set out to walk across good green grass and suddenly find yourself in liquid earth, held together only by the roots of rushes.

Then you are in trouble! Then you need a friend with a rope! Then you'd better not kick or scramble or fight. If you fight the marsh it will fight you back. It will drink you up and swallow you!

Of course, if you are a clever Iceni you will know the paths. You will see how the grasses change to warn you of water under the green. But if you are Roman from over the seas, marching in straight lines with your Roman nose in the air, then in you will go and there you will stay. Even my father, the kindest of men, wouldn't pull a Roman out of a bog.

I like the marsh. It's full of little birds. It's where I go to play when I am tired of grinding the grain to bake our bread, or spinning the wool from the brown Iceni sheep, or cleaning the cooking pots.

I was escaping the cooking pots on the day that I found Honey. Her mother, Little Huff (so called because she liked to huff the dandelion clocks and watch the feathers fly), was calling.

She was calling and calling on the far side of the thorny fence, so deep in reeds and rushes that I only found her by her voice. You cannot follow hoof prints in a marsh, and the reeds are high and springy and close behind you as you walk. It was a wet, tussock-jumping job to find Little Huff. I had to stop and listen, and stop and listen again, but at last I found her, up past

her knees in the marsh. When she saw me she tried to struggle towards me, and sank even deeper.

I couldn't leave her to go for help; I was scared that she would sink even deeper. All I could do was hold her head to stop her panicking, and shout and shout until somebody heard.

For a long time.

Until Brownie, Finn's dog, came pushing through the rushes.

Brownie is clever. He went and fetched Finn.

Finn fetched my father.

My father fetched Uncle Red.

Uncle Red fetched half the village, ropes and wooden poles and rush mats and barley bread with honey on to coax Little Huff quiet.

It took a long, long time before she would follow the men over the rush mats that they laid for her to walk on, but at last they got her out and she was safe.

Then everyone said, "Where's her foal? Where's the foal? Where's your foal, Little Huff?"

There was no sign of a foal anywhere.

Close to Little Huff the marsh was as

blue as the sky. It spread in cool wide pools that had no bottom, only water and muddy water and watery mud.

The men who got Little Huff out told her very kindly that she could have another foal next year and they led her away to the village. But she knew she was leaving her foal behind and she struggled and bit at them. They had such a job making her follow them that they forgot about me. Not even Finn noticed that I had been left behind. He said afterwards that he thought I'd gone ahead to get dry. But I hadn't. I was standing amongst the tall reeds, a little way off and keeping very still.

I was thinking about the foal. Perhaps I could find the foal like I had found Little Huff. That's what I was thinking.

It was quiet when the men were gone, except for the birds and, after a while, another sound that wasn't birds.

Honey, whickering for her mother.

Very carefully I started wading across the blue pools, clutching at the reeds to help me.

It was after dark when they found us, but Honey was not hurt because I held her all the time and I didn't let go until Uncle Red arrived with a lantern and the flat-bottomed boat that he used to hunt ducks in the autumn.

Then there was only room for Honey and Uncle Red in the boat, and I had to wait with the water past my middle. It was so cold I could feel my bones hurting.

But Uncle Red soon came back and he tumbled me into his boat and moments later my father grabbed me out of it and wrapped me in his cloak. I stayed wrapped in my father's cloak across the fields and through the village until we reached the house and the fire. Then hot herb tea with honey in and a great warm fuss.

"What pests these girls are!" said Uncle Red. "The marsh should have swallowed you. Then we'd have some peace!"

But I remembered how quickly he had paddled to me in his little flat boat, calling "Kassy, Kassy, Kassy, I'm here!"

My grandmother got out her best brown pot with leaf patterns on the rim. She said we have to stay friends with the marsh, and that she would give it her pot in the morning, since it had given me back to her.

Everyone nodded, and my father put a coin in the pot too, and then other village people put things in. A handful of grain. A lump of beeswax. An amber bead. Even Finn put in his lucky red bean. "Just in case," said Finn. He said he'd have rescued Honey himself, if he'd been there, only better and quicker and he'd have used a boat.

Uncle Red put a coin in the pot too, and he said if I was his daughter he would beat me with a willow wand, but as I wasn't his daughter he would settle for a hug.

So I did hug him. And Father and Grandmother and Finn. I was so pleased to be out of the cold lapping water, and the sucking grip of the mud. I was glad my grandmother thought of giving the pot to the marsh! It made me feel safer.

Before I went to sleep that night my father said Honey was mine, for ever and ever.

That was the best day of my life. It happened more than two years ago and often, just before I go to sleep, I tell it to myself like a story.

CHAPTER TWO

Every morning the first thing I do is rush outside to see Honey. She lives in the horse runs on the far side of the village. My father is usually there before me, watching.

"You can learn a lot about horses, just by watching them," he says.

We stand side by side and are quiet as they harrumph together or dance away from a shadow or go silent, gazing at something we cannot see.

"Don't you wish you could understand what they are thinking?" I asked my father once.

He looked down at me as if I had said

something quite astonishing.

"Of course I understand what they're thinking!" he said.

"What then?"

"Those two know I'll take one of them for training and they're wondering which. Little Huff saw a bank vole that a weasel had startled. That one gazing is thinking of her foal."

"She hasn't got a foal."

"Her foal is a month away. A month and a day and it will be running beside her!"

"What is Honey thinking?" I asked.

"She's wondering when you'll give her the salt that you are hiding in your hand!" said my father.

"How did you know I had salt in my hand?"

"Honey told me, of course," he said, and laughed at my surprise.

Our village's horses are fit for a queen, that's what we say, and it's true.

Fit for an Iceni queen, fit for Queen Boudica. She came here last summer to look at the bright brown chariot ponies that she always likes the best.

The whole village got ready for that day. The big well was cleaned and the street was swept. Green bracken was piled over the smelly middens where all the village rubbish gets dumped. The children were washed and Uncle Red went from house roof to house roof, patching the thatch. And when Queen Boudica arrived the sky turned twice as blue and the sunlight twice as bright and we took her and her people down to the horse runs in a great chattering crowd.

Queen Boudica was beautiful that day. Her gown was red and her cloak was green and her hair was fiery gold and piled up her head with combs to hold it in place. When the wind caught her cloak she gathered it up and I saw she was wearing gold sandals.

Gold sandals out to the horse runs!

"Ahhh," I breathed, and I laughed out loud because they were so pretty.

Queen Boudica heard me laugh. She looked down at my feet, which were washed but bare, and she looked up at my hair that was blowing in my eyes and then from her own bright hair she took a bronze comb and beckoned me to come close.

Queen Boudica fixed her comb in my tangled hair and then she laughed and I laughed and everyone laughed and Finn's dog Brownie bit off the dog-daisy wreath I had put round his neck and tossed it up in the air.

That's what happened the day I met Queen
Boudica and afterwards my grandmother

untangled the comb from my hair and held it close to her cheek before she put it in a little soft bag to keep it safe for ever.

"You lucky, lucky girl," she said.

"Why is Kassy lucky?" asked Finn.

So then we found out that Finn had missed the whole thing, even when Brownie threw the daisies in the air.

"Too busy staring at the Queen's princesses," said my father. "Which one was it, Finn, the gold or the silver?"

"Silver," said Finn, bravely (although he blushed bright red).

The gold princess was the eldest. She was bigger than me. She was as bright as her mother with the same quick laugh and swift step. Her sister was smaller. She wasn't really silver, but her hair was barley-straw silvery pale and her eyes were silvery grey. She'd fed bread to the horses (which I am not allowed to do) and her face had shone when they nudged her hand for more.

But both princesses were lovely. Gold and silver and lovely.

"Well, why not?" asked my father, hitting Finn between the shoulders almost as hard as he hits Uncle Red. "Why not a princess in the family, eh Red?"

Uncle Red is not a man for talking much about princesses. He rolled his eyes and put his old work tunic on and said he'd been meaning to shift the dung heap for days and Finn could help if he liked.

I love Uncle Red but I can see why no one married him.

Uncle Red is older than my father. He can easily remember the time before the Romans came.

Nobody wants the Romans. Everyone grumbles about them, and detests them, and tells bad stories about them. But Uncle Red acts like every Roman that ever stepped is his own private enemy. They are always on his mind.

The Romans came to our country and they took our towns and they took our land and they took our tracks and made them roads. They marched along those roads in tens and hundreds, and hundreds and more. Armed and smart and ruthless. Some British tribes gave up to them at once, but not the Iceni.

The Iceni never gave up, but still they had to bargain. They had to bargain, or lose everything: the villages and horse runs and fields and Queen Boudica's rule of her people. They had to give up their weapons, and they have to pay the Romans. Tax collectors come to the village. We pay them in coins and horses and anything else that catches their greedy eyes. Last time they took my grandmother's new woven blanket. Food, they like, corn and honey.

But there are ways of making things a little better.

"Pity the poor Roman," says my father, "he's never eaten a honeycomb that some Iceni has not spat on."

The Romans don't stay long near a well-stirred midden either, and the dogs that we tied when Boudica came are not tied when the tax collectors arrive.

My grandmother and my father and my Uncle Red and Finn all say the same thing: "There are no good Romans."

They are wrong. There is one. Not very long ago I met a good Roman and it was because of Honey.

The bigger Honey grew, the prettier and cleverer she became, the more I was afraid of the tax collectors. What if they saw Honey and said, "I'll have her."

The last time they came I was so afraid I hid her.

At the end of the village is a broken old house. It caught fire, like thatched houses often do. Uncle Red patched the burnt thatch but it still smelt bad inside. It came to be used for storing things – wood and an old plough, and a few worn grinding stones. Things like that. That was where I took Honey to hide her and I put mud on her to make her look less lovely than she was. It didn't work very well. Anyone could see that underneath she was shining gold, but I did it anyway. Then I led her into the darkest part of the old house and stayed there with her with my face against her neck. I whispered to her to keep her quiet, "Hush Honey, hush Honey, Honey, Honey, hush!"

When I looked up a Roman tax collector was watching me.

Sometimes the tax collectors speak our language, sometimes their own. This lot spoke ours.

Outside one of them called, "Anything in there?"

Then the Roman watching me smiled and put his finger to his lips and he called back

very clearly to make sure I heard, "Nothing in here. Just a little dirty honey!"

And then he was gone.

One good Roman.

When I told about it afterwards nobody would believe me. They didn't even want to listen. "Stop that talk!" said Uncle Red, so fiercely that I did.

I stopped talking, but I didn't forget. Whenever I notice the empty house I remember and I smile.

CHAPTER THREE

Something terrible has happened.

One evening a messenger arrived at our village. He came galloping. He flung himself off his horse shouting to the people. We were in the house, eating our evening meal, but we saw him through the open door.

My father looked across to my grandmother. Uncle Red jumped to his feet. Finn said, "Wait! I'm not being left!" and then all three were gone.

Finn's dog, Brownie, ran after them.

They left their suppers. Barley broth with greens in it. Some fish Finn caught when he should have been in the field strips. New bread with the first honey.

That was the last time my family sat together and talked of little things; where the bees had been, and if I had washed the greens for the soup carefully or did they have to watch out for caterpillars, like had happened the day before. Finn described an enormous fish he had caught that unluckily got away. Uncle Red told about a dream he had the night before, where a great black dragon was woven into his thatching.

"Not all dreams are for telling," my grandmother said sternly, and Finn whispered to me, "Uncle Red has beetles in his hair, that's what his dream means!" and my father overheard and burst into laughter.

It's a good thing you don't know when last times are last times.

After the messenger came, Grandmother and I were left alone. I wanted to run after Finn and my father and Uncle Red, but Grandmother wouldn't let me. I had to stay and clear the bowls and wash the soup pot. Then, as soon as they were clean, my grandmother got out her comb (her TERRIBLE bone comb!) and said, "Kassy, you were speaking of beetles in the hair..."

"Finn was, not me!" I protested. "And not in my hair! In Uncle Red's!"

But it was no use. Grandmother started with the tangles on my shoulders and worked her way up towards my ears. She had me halfway untangled before I fell asleep on my stool. I only knew I was asleep when I toppled off and found Grandmother pushing me into bed.

Every time I woke that night I heard mens' voices outside. Angry men's voices, all night.

The first strange thing was the baking.

All night my grandmother baked. Barley bread and corn bread in flat round loaves. In all the other houses the women were baking too. At daylight bread appeared outside the door of every home, piled on tables, cooling. I had never seen so much bread before. Indoors, the women were still turning loaves on the hearths.

They baked enough bread for an army.

In the morning the rider was gone, taking the news to more villages.

Soon it would be their last times too.

As soon as it was light my father went out to the horse runs as he always did, but Uncle Red did not go with him. Uncle Red was going mad among the rooftops.

For twenty years Uncle Red had thatched the roofs of our village, and now he was pulling them apart. He was not the only person pulling things apart. Finn was unstacking the wood pile by the wasps' nest. Wasps built new nests in that dark corner every year and Uncle Red would never have them killed. Uncle Red liked wasps. He left them in the thatches too. When children were stung and ran wailing to their mothers, Uncle Red didn't care at all.

"Be thankful it was only a wasp," he would say.

The wasps by the woodpile were in a seething temper, now their home was being disturbed at last. Theirs was nothing compared to Finn's temper though. He was working all by himself, and he looked awful. His face was as wooden as the logs he was hurling aside.

Other boys were unstacking woodpiles too, and digging behind middens. They mostly looked scared. All the big girls were doing the same boring thing. Grinding grain for more baking.

Grinding and grinding.

It makes a sharp pain between your

shoulders.

It was after dark when I saw the first
sword.

Finn was holding it, and his blue friendly
eyes were like blue stones.

Where did they come from, these swords?
These spears? How could they be here, all
in a day? I asked Uncle Red and he looked
at me and scratched his thatched head.

Oh.

Hidden from the Romans for all these years. Guarded by wasps and dogs and cunning. Not just in this village, but in all the Iceni villages and farmsteads and huts, all through the country.

In all the other Iceni villages, are they taking down wood piles and digging by middens and opening the thatch? Are they grinding and baking and sharpening blades and looking at each other with eyes like stones?

No one will tell me anything. Not my father or Finn or my grandmother or anyone I catch hold of, until I catch Uncle Red.

Sharpening swords.

"Why won't anyone tell me anything?" I demand.

"Because," said Uncle Red, "what you don't know can't be frightened out of you." Then his eyes flick me a look.

"Something terrible has happened," I say.

"Has it?" asks Uncle Red, feeling a blade with his thumb.

"That messenger rode a bright brown horse," I remember out loud.

"Good fast horses, those brown ones," said Uncle Red.

"Queen Boudica has horses like that."

"Fit for a queen, those horses," agrees Uncle Red, and again his eyes flick me a look.

"Something terrible has happened to Queen Boudica," I say.

Uncle Red glances at me.

"Was it the Romans?"

"Was it who?"

"Did they hurt her? Did they hurt her gold and silver girls?"

Uncle Red looks carefully along a blade and then makes it sing in the air. He nods his head slowly.

"Is she dead?"

"No, she's not dead," said Uncle Red. "She's alive. She's angry. And that's all you need to know."

I think I must have been the last person in the village to understand what was going to happen next. My Uncle Red, my father, Finn, my village, they were going to take those swords and they were going to kill people. That's what swords are for. Killing people. Enemies.

The Iceni are summoning an army.

When Finn said he was going with them I couldn't bear it. I held his tunic in my fists and said, "You can't."

"I can," said Finn. He shoved me away and went off to Uncle Red.

Uncle Red put an arm across Finn's shoulders. He hugged Finn to him. Uncle

Red! When did Uncle Red do a thing like that!

"They've had it now," said Uncle Red. "They're finished. That's it."

Finn lifted up his head and nodded.

They are talking about the Romans, I know.

The Romans are our enemies. They took our country and now they have done something terrible to our Queen. They have gone too far. They have had it now. They're finished. That's it. Everyone says the same, not just Uncle Red.

Boudica is on fire for revenge. The village is on fire for revenge. The Iceni are on fire for revenge. There are hidden swords and spears. There are long-planned secrets. There are thousands of people as angry as my Uncle Red.

Uncle Red shouldn't be worried about

anything frightening me. What could be more frightening than Uncle Red, glaring and growling and sharpening swords by firelight?

Firelight.

"We'll need fire to follow the blades," said Uncle Red to my father as I ground and ground and ground the grain to make more loaves.

Oh no! Not fire! Who fights with fire? I've seen fire. I've seen a thatch burn and crumble and fall on the home beneath.

The poor Romans, if the Iceni arrive at their houses with fire. The poor, poor Romans.

Somebody should warn them.

I said that aloud and my family heard me.

"Kassy," said my father in a voice he had never used before. "Come here."

So I did.

"Don't you say those words again," said my father. "Don't you think them. Don't you show them in your eyes. Do you understand?"

"No," I said.

"There are no good Romans," said my father.

"There's one," I said. "Don't you remember? When Honey and I hid?"

Then Uncle Red stood over me and he said, "Girl, there are people in the village who would kill you for those words you said just now."

"She's a child," said my grandmother, and now she was standing too.

"Kill you," repeated Uncle Red, and in front of my father and my grandmother and Finn he put his thumbs on my throat. "Like this," he said, and pressed until I squeaked with fear.

My father roared and leapt at him but my grandmother got there first and untangled their arms and their angry bones and she said, "Red's right. Better she knows."

I was sent out of the way to cry if I wanted, but I didn't. I went out into the dark and across to the horse runs. There I whistled and Honey came running.

I stood for a long time with my arms around Honey's neck.

I wish that messenger had never ridden to our village but I didn't tell Honey that. I didn't tell Honey anything.

I had no words left to speak.

Uncle Red had seen to that. With his thumbs he had silenced me, inside and out. So I pushed from my mind the thought of the good Roman who had saved Honey for me, and of the good Roman's friends, if he had any friends, and of his brother and daughter and son and his mother, if he had those people, and his dog like Brownie, if he had a dog. I pushed away his merry smile when he said, "Just a little dirty honey."

You wouldn't think it was possible if you'd seen as many swords as I had seen that day, or the wagons loaded with firewood for after the swords.

But I did.

That evening, a dark cloak of Iceni swept up to our village. Men and boys and swords and spears. Wagons laden with bread and wood and cloth to bind wounds. Whole families sometimes.

It was like the spring rains, when a small flood joins a big flood and the water spreads over the land.

Queen Boudica was leading the great spreading rabble. I glimpsed our bright brown horses racing with her chariot. Her golden hair flew out like flames as she passed.

I didn't know there were so many people in the world.

So many horses.

So many swords.

CHAPTER FOUR

Now they are gone.

The Iceni are going to the city of Colchester. That used to be our city until the Romans took it and made it their centre.

When the Iceni reach Colchester they are going to kill every Roman in it and burn it to the ground. Then they will move on to London and do the same. And then on to the next place after that.

Our village feels as hollow as an eggshell when the bird has hatched and flown. There is hardly anyone left. Some very young children, and some very old people. Even the dogs have followed their masters. Except for the oldest and stiffest, the village is empty of dogs. People left behind stare at each other. I am not the only person who cannot find a single word to say.

"Look after your grandmother," said my father, that last night. "You are the best girl in the world."

"Look after your grandmother," said Uncle Red. "I didn't hurt you. I would never hurt you."

"Look after our grandmother," said Finn, hugging me. "I'm sorry."

I have stopped saying words since those thumbs on my throat, so I didn't ask, "Sorry for what?"

I soon found out.

My grandmother is already restacking what's left of the woodpile. Covering the midden. Now she's on the roof, untangling the torn thatch. She says she is getting ready for when they all come back. Slowly, slowly, the few people left in the village are beginning to stir. We stand close together, gathering up what's left of our world to feel safe. Babies and old people and a few tired dogs and, I think, Honey!

I'll fetch Honey! She can live here in the village with Grandmother and me!

So I go racing down to the horse runs.

The horse runs are as empty as the village. I whistle and I whistle but Honey doesn't come.

Where is she? She was much too young to be taken on such a hard journey! She has never carried anyone heavier than me.

I whistle more, again and again, and at last I hear a reply. A whicker. A pony whicker. And hooves.

Slow hooves though.

It is Old Flax.

Fat Old Flax. The barrel-shaped old horse that my father always laughed at and kept for luck.

Now I understand why Finn said sorry. He was taking Honey.

Honey, taken to war.

There is not much left to eat in the village, but what there is my grandmother has charge of. She has untangled the muddle that is left. The very old people are minding the babies. The oldest of all are grinding grain. There is a fire going and the tired dogs are resting in the warmth. I see someone has brought water. Grandmother has just remembered the fish trap in the river. She doesn't need me to look after her.

Good.

Because I am going after Honey.

Honey does need me to look after her. She will be afraid. I know what she will do. She will run away the first chance she gets, and Honey is clever. I don't know how Finn caught her once. He won't catch her twice.

Honey will be lost.

As soon as I had thought all this I couldn't wait. I ached to be away.

What do you need for such a journey?

A blanket.

Some bread.

Old Flax.

It will have to be Old Flax. That fat, biting, flea-bitten old horse! But his four legs will be faster than my two. I have a blanket of my own. I'll take that. There was a batch of loaves that got burnt and were set aside and forgotten. I'll take them too.

It was easy. This was my plan:

Bread in a sack.

Blanket on Old Flax.

Leave.

I am going to follow the Iceni army to Colchester.

But first I go and stand very close to my Grandmother, so close that I can feel her bones.

"Kassy," she says with her hand on my tangles, and for a moment we are still. We face south. South is the way they went. Colchester is south, and now that is the only direction that any one can look. The round circle of the world has closed like a fan to a line that points one way.

Every moment that I stand close to my grandmother the Iceni are travelling further along that line.

I didn't tell her I was going, so she didn't tell me to stay.

CHAPTER FIVE

So this is the road to Colchester and I am already further from the village than I have ever been before.

There is no chance of me getting lost on the way. The army has left a trail as wide as a field. They have spread across the old track and flooded out over the land on either side. The ground is crushed by their passing.

Old Flax is a terrible horse to ride! He does everything possible to stop me. He lifts his long leathery lip and lunges at me with yellow-grey teeth. He twists when I mount and tries to jerk me to the ground. He grinds my legs against tree trunks to try and rub me off. He would roll and squash me flat if he wasn't too fat to roll.

He is much too fat, twice as wide as Honey, and he is stone hard to sit on, a jolting bag of stones. I bit my tongue very hard the first time he trotted. Then he stopped very suddenly and my face hit his neck and my nose started bleeding.

But I ride him anyway.

As I travel, the trail spreads wider and wider. Other villages are gathering to join the Iceni host. I pass a circle of huts, very small and poor, but they are quiet and empty.

On that first day I see a little dog. He is the first victim of this war.

He is a rough-coated little dog and he has been kicked by a horse. His back is broken. His eyes look at me, but he cannot move.

What shall I do with this dog?

I tie Old Flax to a hawthorn tree while

I look at him. I have to watch Old Flax too, because he is trying to bite through the rope. The little dog is panting. I offer him some of my burnt bread but he does not take it, even when I push it right to his mouth. His eyes do not move from mine.

Water, I think.

I haven't any water but there is rain water standing in a nearby hollow. I haven't anything to carry water so I have to empty my bread from my bread sack (taking care that Old Flax cannot reach the loaves) and then soak the sack in the marshy water.

Then I carry it to the little dog and drip the water over his tongue. He licks his nose. I do it again. Is it better for him? I don't know.

The third time I bring the little dog water he doesn't lick his nose. The drips pool around his head. His eyes stay on mine but their brightness fades and goes, like a wet stone drying in the sun.

It was very hard to leave him. It was like leaving Grandmother all over again. I spent too long stroking his rough little head.

Oh, I was lonely that first day. It would have been more than I could bear, if I hadn't had Old Flax.

Old Flax! What a horse! No wonder they left him behind. When I left the little dog at last and went back to untie him from the thorn tree he wouldn't move a step. He stood like a stone horse. But I petted him, and rubbed his ears and climbed on his back and shook the reins.

Then he moved. He walked right into the hawthorn tree and tangled my hair in its branches.

Ouch!

OUCH!

A whole clump of my hair tugged from my head by the thorny branches!

It hurt so much I felt my head to see if I had a bald patch in the middle like my father does in his.

I had. I could feel it.

But Old Flax didn't care.

I got off and tried to lead him and it was like trying to lead the wood pile. I held out bread to tempt him. He walked two steps forward to get the bread and four steps back to chew it.

It got to be night.

In the dark I tied Old Flax back to the hawthorn tree and then I gathered a bundle of long grass, as big as I could, and piled it underneath. I spread my blanket on top of the pile and lay down on my blanket under my cloak. I couldn't help wondering if Old Flax would trample over me, but he didn't. Perhaps he couldn't be bothered. He ate the grass like I'd hoped he would, and pulling it from underneath me stopped him chewing through his rope. It was nice to know he was there while I slept.

Sort of slept.

It didn't feel like sleep, but it must have been, because at dawn I woke up. My hair was soaked in dew and more tangled than ever but I had got through the dark night and it was morning. I ate some of my bread.

My bread is wonderful. It tastes of home. I don't care that it is burnt. I like the burnt bits best. When I get back to the village I will always burn the bread a little. I think it is better that way. Old Flax likes my burnt bread too. He grabs when I give him a piece. I cannot give him much because he can eat grass, but I can't.

Before it was properly light I was back on Old Flax and this time he went forward when I wanted him to. I think I have learned something about this old horse, which is that he will only start once a day.

I think that's quite funny and clever. I wish I could tell Finn.

I am starting to love Old Flax. You have to love something. I do, anyway. So even though Old Flax bites my shoulders and hits me with his tail, I love him. I don't think he loves me though. This morning he flicked out a back leg and kicked me right over.

Poor Old Flax. He doesn't like this journey. What he would like to do is shake me off and eat up all my bread and then head straight home.

Well, he can't, but I have found something Old Flax likes. He likes to be rubbed on his back and neck with a handful of rough grass. He lets me do that as we jog along together.

On the second day of riding I didn't dare to get off once, in case Old Flax wouldn't start again. I was so tired that I fell asleep as I rode, with my head on his neck, and my fingers wound tight in his mane. We passed more empty huts, and one place where small children were standing outside. They hid at first when they saw us, and then as we got closer they came out again and stared, sucking their fingers. After we passed they took their fingers out of their mouths and called.

"Stop! Come to us!" they called, but we didn't stop.

That day I met more Iceni, riding late after the war host. Four men came galloping hard down the track behind us. As they came up they spread out on either side and rose on their horses to look at Old Flax and me. They stared.

I sat up as straight as I could and tried to look fearless and old. I pointed my arm to the south, straight, as if it held a sword. The men looked at each other, and shook their heads.

Mad, said their looks.

Then they shrugged, shrugging off the thought of me I suppose, and turned their eyes on Old Flax. I could see they were thinking: "Shall we take that horse?"

That frightened me.

What could I do if they took Old Flax? Walk?

Could I walk all the way to Colchester?

I held my breath while I waited to see what they would do.

It was as if Old Flax understood. He looked at those four staring, unfriendly men and he dropped his head and lifted his tail.

Old Flax made a rude noise from under

his tail and suddenly there was a very bad smell. I know he did it on purpose. Then he stretched back his head and showed the men the angry red whites of his eyes. He lifted his lip and bit at the air with his old yellow teeth.

"Useless," said one of the men, and the other three nodded and said, "Useless."

Oh, clever Old Flax! No wonder my father laughed at him and kept him for luck.

When I stop tonight I will give Old Flax a whole hunk of bread! The men rode on and I was so glad to breathe again.

Then one of them turned and wheeled back. He smiled at me with his teeth showing and he called, "Girl! There are children back there in the huts! Go there! Go back to the children, you girl. You hear?"

I nodded.

Then he wheeled round and was gone.

As if I would go back!

Before I knew one more thing about those men, I knew I didn't like them. I am learning new things all the time. Already I knew that you didn't have to hate someone, even if they were Roman. Now I knew that I didn't have to like them, even if they were Iceni. Those men would have taken Old Flax and left me to walk. No one from our village would have done such a thing, but they were hard, cold strangers.

Later that day I found what those men did after they rode away from me.

It was evening when I saw the bundles. They were not on the straight track south, they were a little way to the side. Two large dark bundles. I thought of all the things that I wished I had brought when I hurried away from the village. A warmer cloak, something to carry water. A spare rope to lead Honey.

Bread. I'd eaten as little as possible, but even so I hadn't much left in my sack of burnt bread.

So I turned Old Flax towards those bundles.

They were men. I couldn't believe it at first. I stared and stared at the first dead people I had ever seen.

Two men with grey hair, and short Roman tunics. They had fallen on their faces, running. They had been speared from behind not long before.

Those four riders must have done it.

Old Flax skittered sideways when he saw them and I nearly fell. Old Flax's lip was curling and his ears were laid flat back. He ran away down the track, faster than I had known Old Flax could run.

He ran north and I couldn't turn him.

We have wasted too much time, I thought, as I lay under my cloak that night. Time with the little dog and now time travelling backwards. In future we will go straight on, not stopping and not turning aside for anything.

I am so hungry I have to hide the bread from myself or else I will eat it all. I wish I could eat grass like Old Flax. Crunch,

crunch, crunch! He makes it sound delicious! I fall asleep thinking of cooked beans and porridge. Of baked apples and honey. Of roast meat and new bread and soup with peas in it. Of eggs and milk. Of Finn's big fish that got away.

I wonder what Finn is thinking of now.

I began to lose count of days after that one. It is no use remembering what I saw. At night we rested. At daylight we went south. I didn't turn aside to look at anything, ever. Honey was growing further and further away. It began to feel like a dream where I would always be riding Old Flax southwards.

I wished Old Flax were faster. I wished he would gallop and gallop. I wished I could see the war host just ahead. I think Honey would be one of the last of them, struggling to keep up. How fast could she travel with Finn on her back?

Not very fast, I hope.

Perhaps we will come across them, camped in some quiet place, Honey and Finn and Father and Uncle Red and Brownie all together. Then I will whistle and Honey come running and bump me with her bee-velvet nose. Brownie will bounce around me, wagging his tail, but perhaps Finn will be angry. He won't want to swap Honey for Old Flax.

Uncle Red will roar.

Father will gather me up.

Anytime now, perhaps I will see them again!

What I hope most, is that Father will make Finn travel back home with me. That's my best hope as I jog along. To meet them at a quiet time. To be sent back to Grandmother with Finn.

And Brownie.

Could it really happen? Would Queen Boudica allow it?

Yes, she would. Queen Boudica is kind. Perhaps she will remember the bronze comb that she put in my hair. Also, she knows about horses. She won't want Honey to be hurt and frightened. Now I have a very good idea that makes me feel much better. I will say to her (politely, very, very politely) "Queen Boudica I will give you Honey. Send us home now, with Finn and Brownie, and when you have conquered and when you come home and when Honey is grown I will give her to you. Please Queen Boudica. Do you remember the day in our village when the sky turned twice as blue and Brownie threw the daisies and you gave me your comb? When the days are like that again, I'll bring you Honey, and you can have her for ever, and all her foals too."

I practise this speech in my head as we travel along, half asleep, and I eat my bread in the evening.

We must be getting close now.

My bread is all gone.

For some time we have been passing burned farmsteads – Roman farms, not Iceni. Square, high walls and roofs with tiles. We have passed more bundles like the ones the four men left. Now the land looks like a great rough plough has passed over it. All the green has turned to black. All the trees are broken. All the buildings are black too.

The air begins to smell of burning. The sky to the south is darkness, even at midday. There are no stars at night.

CHAPTER SIX

The last day of riding was through ruin. I wish I hadn't seen the things that I saw that day. The small horse stumbling with the broken leg. The smashed cart with the two children. That must have been their father underneath, but where was their mother? Who scattered their belongings after they died? Who broke their cooking pots and tore their blankets? What good did it do? And the old woman beside the wall. Much older than my grandmother.

I didn't know it would be like this.

I keep looking for Finn.

Now I have come to the city.

This is it. This is Colchester. But there is no living thing to be seen. I cannot hear even a bird. There is no one here.

This is what I see:

A huge, stone-walled town, much, much bigger than our village. The walls are broken, tumbled as if the earth had shaken underneath. I can see burnt rooftops beyond the wall. Sky shows in the gaps between the timbers.

There are gates in the wall, thick arches of stone. The gate nearest to Old Flax and me is blocked with fallen stone and burnt wood. The whole town has been burnt and there is such a bitter smell of burning in the air that I can taste it in my mouth, and my eyes sting with pain.

As if in a dream, Old Flax and I circle the broken walls. It is warm here. The stones are still warm from the flames.

Who did this?

It doesn't look like men did this.

Was this my father, Uncle Red and Finn? Was this Queen Boudica with her bright brown horses?

Where is everyone?

Where is Honey?

Where are the brave Iceni?

Where are the terrible Romans?

Halfway round our circle of the city, Old Flax and I find a great arched gate in the wall that isn't broken. It's open and we can see inside.

It is like looking into the end of the world. I'm not going in there. Honey cannot be in there. Nothing alive could be in there.

And then I see that I am wrong.

There is a small movement. I have been seen. A little cat comes tiptoeing along by a wall towards me. I can see that it is terribly frightened. Each step that it takes is careful.

A little black cat.

I slide off Old Flax and hold out my hand. The little cat comes to me and rubs its round head against my shaking legs.

Old Flax is too tired to bother to move. I can hear my heart banging.

The little black cat has a white star-shaped mark on her face. Still white, in all this blackness. Her eyes are the shining green of sunlight through leaves. She stretches and arches around my feet. Will she let me pick her up?

Yes.

I tuck her under my cloak and she begins to make a new sound. Like running water but softer. Like a bumble bee but sweeter.

Purring.

It is very late in the day and Old Flax needs water. Looking south, I see the road running away before me. There is a small arched stone shelter beside the road. I saw a place like that before, on the journey down. The Romans build them. The other was sheltering the water tank of a well. Perhaps this is another. Perhaps we will find water there. Anyway, that's where we are going, the little cat and Old Flax and me.

Poor Old Flax. I lead him, and he follows like a tired dog. We move like one animal together now, Old Flax and I. We try not to look around us too much.

Dead men look very alike I think. Roman and Iceni, dark and fair, curled or lying sprawled. I haven't seen a small gold horse. I don't want to see a brown dog. I don't know what I would do if I did. Would I look, and find Finn?

I think these things to stop me thinking of water because suddenly I know how much I need that arch to be a well.

Water, water, water. My throat is ash dry and burning.

And it is a well.

Who found this water? Who built this

well? Iceni or Roman, I thank them from the whole of me. There is clear water in cool stone, and the little cat drinks and Old Flax drinks and I drink and drink and drink and then we look around.

The land is growing darker. There is deep shadow now beside the city walls and in the shadow a boy is moving.

A boy, not a man.

A boy the size of Finn, but not Finn. Thin as a willow wand with shaggy dark hair. He leads a dark grey pony.

Old Flax and I don't make a sound.

We lose sight of him between heaps of stone and rubble, and then we see him again. He is creeping to the South Gate. He moves like a boy locked in fear. Sometimes he stands so still that I cannot see him at all. He is gentle with his pony. I see him smooth his hand along its neck. Then he becomes lost in the darkness around the South Gate.

Has he gone through the gate? That was brave, if he has. I wouldn't go through that gate.

The little cat is folded snug in my cloak. I hold it tight, and with my other hand I lead Old Flax forward. We have to leave the well anyway, because surely the boy will want it himself before dark, and then he will find us there. But we make our way back northwards again, towards the gate that has swallowed the boy and his pony. We can hear his voice.

The boy is calling. He is calling gently there in the warm burnt ruins. "Stella, Stella, veni Stella!"

'Stella' is star. I know that. Who would call for a star in such a dark place? But the little cat is struggling under my cloak, and all at once I understand! This boy has come for his cat!

I am so relieved that it feels as if I just had walked into sunlight.

Iceni or Roman, this is a boy like me, and he has come to find his cat, just as I came to find Honey. So I start to run towards the South Gate, clutching the cat, tugging Old Flax, forgetting to be quiet. I didn't think how the sound of me rushing across in the dark would frighten the boy, but of course it did. The gateway was silent when I arrived. It was silent while I stood hidden in the shadows and waited.

Then there was a small whicker. The voice of a horse, and I know that call!

I lost my words under Uncle Red's thumbs, but I didn't lose my whistle. I whistle and whistle, and the pony replies.

Just like Honey!

But Honey was gold, and this pony is dark grey. I know I must be dreaming but when I rub my eyes the pony is still there. It is Honey, not golden but ash grey.

My little dirty Honey! She comes dancing out of the shadows and behind her she pulls a Roman boy. He has my Honey safe and I have his little cat Stella tangled in my cloak.

So we swap.

I knew there were good Romans.

CHAPTER SEVEN

The Roman boy holds his cat against his face. My cheek is pressed on Honey's neck. The murmurs which the Roman boy makes to his cat and I make to Honey have the same sound.

Old Flax doesn't like to be ignored for so long. He fidgets and bites at my shoulder and blows hard through his nose. When he blows through his nose there is a terrible sound from the city behind us. A great groaning screech, and a huge rumble. The smash of falling stone, the long thunder of tumbling roof tiles. The Roman boy and I grab the horses and run and run and run.

We run north from the city, tumbling and stumbling in the dark, north and north and north until our legs refuse to do it any more.

When we can't run any longer, we walk, and when we can't walk, we stagger, the boy leading Old Flax, me leading Honey. I remember being bowed by the weight of my head on my shoulders but I don't remember anything more. I don't remember falling asleep but I must have done.

When I woke the Roman boy was looking at me. Black eyes.

The little cat was beside him. Honey and Old Flax were tied to a broken tree. In daylight I could see a smudge or two of gold through the ashes on Honey's coat. Old Flax was grey with ashes too, just like her. So was I. So was the Roman boy.

I wonder when that happened.

I didn't notice before.

The boy had been waiting for me to wake. He had one hand behind his back. When he saw me looking he drew it out. He was holding a round flat loaf.

I was so hungry I swallowed and swallowed. The boy broke the loaf in two halves. He held them up, measuring which was biggest.

He gave the biggest to me.

I wonder who baked that loaf for him.

We ate together, biting our bread with our eyes on each other's faces. When it was gone we both stroked the cat. The boy pointed to the cat and said, "Stella," and I nodded to show that I understood he meant her name.

Then he pointed to himself and said, "Marcus."

Then he pointed to me.

I made a sound but it wasn't my name. I tried again and it was a croak. The boy pointed to Honey and I whispered at last, "Honey."

Honey.

Honey.

My voice is free! I have words to speak again! I point to myself and say, "Kassy" and to the boy and say "Marcus". I name Honey again, and Stella and Old Flax. I chew imaginary bread and say, "Thank you."

The boy nods.

Marcus has nothing and no one left except Stella his cat. I know because he told me. He held his hands out flat to the sky and two tears showed in his black Roman eyes. Marcus has more bread though. Three loaves. He brought them out and laid them on the ground between us.

I have no bread left, but I have somewhere to go and somebody left. I have my grandmother. I didn't even say goodbye. I want her more than anything else in the world right now.

I know where I'm going. I'm going home.

I point to myself, Kassy, and I point north to tell Marcus.

Marcus nods again, to show he that he understands that I, Kassy, am going north. I still have somewhere to go.

Then Marcus passes me two loaves of

bread.

Thank you, Marcus.

Oh, this is going to take some untangling! But I try.

I take the Roman boy's hand. I say, "Kassy and Marcus" and I point my other hand north.

The two tears spill down the Roman boy's face.

CHAPTER EIGHT

That first day we hardly moved, except to leave the churned trail of the army and cross to the unspoilt countryside in the east. There we found a patch of scrubby land where blackberry bushes grew. The berries were purple and black and we ate them in handfuls. They made my sore throat feel better. There were nut bushes too, with green nuts in clusters. I filled my empty bread sack with green nuts for the journey home.

For most of that day we rested. We slept and woke, picked berries and nuts, and dozed and woke again. In between I tried to ask questions, and Marcus tried to answer them.

You would think that would be impossible, because Marcus spoke not one word of my language, and I spoke not one word of his.

But the Roman boy has an amazing thing! So simple, so clever! When I get home, if I get home, I will make one for myself. One for myself, and one for Finn. Finn would love it!

It's small, the size of two folded hands. Two flat thin wooden boards joined along one edge. It opens like a butterfly's wings and then closes shut again. When it is closed shut you cannot see that inside the wooden boards are shallow frames and the frames are filled with wax. Beeswax. There is a layer of beeswax on each board and a sharp bronze stick on a leather thong.

Often Finn and I have drawn pictures on smoothed earth with a stick. Pictures to show each other where we had gone, a fish for the river, a round hut for home. Once Finn drew Father with his hair all fallen off. Once I drew Uncle Red dancing on a roof.

So I knew about pictures.

Now Marcus takes his sharp bronze stick and makes pictures on the beeswax. He carves the wax like back in the village my father used to carve wood. But the wax is better than wood because you can carve it again and again. You can smooth it and make a new picture.

That was how Marcus answered my questions. With pictures.

That is the way I found out how he came to have Honey.

The story of Honey and Marcus was long. I had to wait to see it all drawn.

First Marcus drew people. A man with two crutches under his arm. He hopped on one leg. A woman holding bread in her hands. A boy with a cat.

His father. His mother. Marcus and Stella.

Marcus drew the city, the walls and the rooftops. He drew a road from the city leading down to a river. He drew boats on the river. Not little boats like the one Uncle Red used to rescue Honey and me from the marsh. Big boats.

Then Marcus pointed.

He showed me that his mother and father and Stella the cat were in the city.

He showed me that he was out of the city. He was beside a boat.

What was he doing there?

Marcus drew big pots by the boats. He pointed to show me the pots came out of the boats. He pointed to his father to show the pots belonged to him.

Marcus counted the pots. Four pots. He made a mark in the wax for each pot.

So I understood that Marcus the Roman boy went down to the river to watch the pots being unloaded from the boats and to count them. They were for his father. He went instead of his father because his father had crutches and couldn't walk well.

But what about Honey?

"Honey?" I asked.

Marcus held up his hand to show I must wait to hear about Honey. He smoothed the wax and began to draw more.

Here was the city and the walls again. Here was the gate where I found Stella. Many, many people now came running from the gate.

They ran towards the river.

Marcus stopped drawing and pointed at me.

Me?

He nodded. He spoke a word I knew.

"Iceni," said Marcus.

Oh.

That's why the people were running.

I turned away from Marcus. I didn't want to look at him. I went to hug Honey and to rub Old Flax with grass. I picked a handful of nuts from a bush. My mind was all a tangle. I was ashamed.

But I wanted to shout too.

I wanted to shout questions to Marcus.

What about the tax collectors coming to

our village? What about Queen Boudica and her gold and silver girls? What about our stolen horses and honeycombs and woven blankets and bags of coins? What about our stolen land?

I didn't go back to Marcus for a long time.

The next picture Marcus drew was of a boy like himself. The boy was trying to pull Marcus into a boat. The boy's eyes are wide open and his mouth is wide open as if he is shouting. What is he telling Marcus?

Marcus draws a terrible picture.

The man with the crutches is lying on the ground. His eyes are closed as if he is sleeping but he isn't sleeping. He is stabbed with a spear.

Marcus draws broken pots. He draws his mother beside them. Her eyes are closed too.

When I look at Marcus his hands are over his face. He rocks like he is blowing in the wind.

What can I do? What can I do?

I pick up Stella who is prowling amongst the blackberry bushes and I carry her to Marcus and I put her on his knees. He holds her tight against his chest.

I pick blackberries for Marcus and I lay them on a leaf to carry them. They are perfect berries. I checked each one to make sure. I put them beside Marcus.

"I'm sorry," I say.

I rub his back and he lets me.

After a while he lifts his head and begins to draw again.

Now the city is burning. Smoke rises under Marcus's hand. It billows and spreads. It covers the whole of the wax.

Out of the smoke a pony comes running. Honey.

I laugh out loud to see her.

Honey! There is Honey running out of the smoke, out of the wax, before my eyes! How frightened she is! Her ears are laid back. Her eyes stare.

Honey runs to the river and there she stops.

Marcus stands up and shows me how he called to Honey then. He holds out his hand. "Veni, veni, veni!" he calls and Honey comes to him likes she comes to my whistle. He rubs her neck and pats her shoulder, and she leans her head against him. That's how she came to him out of the smoke, frightened and he comforted her.

Honey and Marcus, lost in the smoke together. They drink from the river. Marcus sleeps. When he wakes he remembers that his mother is dead and his father is dead. His home is burnt. Nothing is left.

Except maybe one thing.

Stella.

In the quiet of the evening, Marcus goes back to look for Stella. There he is on the dark wax in front of me: a boy and a pony.

Then Marcus puts down his wax boards and nods at me. That is the end, his nod says. All the rest you know! You found Stella. I found Honey. He points to Honey in the wax. He has answered all my questions.

No he hasn't! No he hasn't!

Now it is my turn to draw.

I draw a boy, my brother Finn, riding on Honey's back. I draw his curly head and his dog Brownie running beside him. I push the picture to Marcus and I point to them both. Did Marcus see them?

Marcus looks very sadly at me and he shakes his head. No Finn. No Brownie. He takes the wax back to draw more smoke. Smoke everywhere.

No use then, to draw Father or Uncle Red, or Queen Boudica and the bright brown horses?

No.

Now it is my turn to cover my face with my hands and Marcus's turn to put blackberries beside me and give me Stella to hold and rub my back.

There are still so many questions I would like to ask Marcus, and there must be just as many that he wants to ask me, but that is enough for one day. I bring out one of the loaves that he gave to me the night before. We will have to make this bread last at least another four days, but I break off two pieces and I hold them up to measure them.

I give the biggest one to Marcus and he smiles.

Marcus folds away the waxed wooden boards that have told us so much. Bread and blackberries and warm afternoon sunshine. After a while we sleep.

When I woke it was evening. In the north the sky was clear and there was Honey, with Old Flax. I had found her. Honey was safe.

I began to feel better.

I cannot guess how this will end. A Roman boy in an Iceni village, if there is an Iceni village left for us to find. Who knows what will be left, or who will return? The Iceni have burned Colchester and moved on to the next city. They have had the revenge they rode to find with Boudica.

But somewhere out there is a huge Roman army.

They will want their own revenge now.

Come home, Father! Come home, Finn! Finn, you will like Marcus, you couldn't not like Marcus!

Come home, Uncle Red!

But although one half of me is afraid of what Uncle Red will do when he finds out

I have brought a Roman boy back to our village, the other half of me guesses that I will never see Uncle Red again.

Will anyone return?

Will my father's huge smile light our house as he comes in from the fields?

Will Finn and Brownie race each other back from the river?

Will Boudica come next spring to visit the horses in the horse runs?

Will the memories of these past days ever untangle from my mind?

Marcus and I have seen too much. We have been too frightened. We have been too sad.

We need my grandmother.

"Hurry! Hurry!" I say to Marcus and he understands at once and picks up Stella and tucks her under his cloak. We gather the nuts and the loaves of bread. We fetch Old Flax and Honey.

In the village the evening bread will be baked and cooling. The babies will be sleeping and the old dogs will be lying close to the fire. My grandmother will be thinking of the next work to begin.

Perhaps she is thinking of me.

I'm sure she is thinking of me

Old Flax likes going north and he lets Marcus ride. We will travel by night and hide by day, because we are a Roman boy and an Iceni girl, and we are friends and people will not understand.

A clean wind is blowing. The sky is clear, and there are stars again.

You would think, after all that has happened, even the stars would have fled from their places in the sky. But they haven't. They are still there. They still shine in their lovely patterns.

Thank you, Grandmother, for showing me the stars.

There is the North Star, high overhead. I untangle it from the night sky and point it out to Marcus, and that's how we find our way home.

EPILOGUE

The Iceni army burnt Colchester, and killed as many people as they could. It is difficult to know how many that was, because some people did manage to escape.

The Roman citizens knew that the Iceni were angry. When the news came of what had happened to Boudica and her daughters, people probably guessed what would happen next. We know about the fire because it left behind a thick layer of deep red burnt ash. That layer is still there. People excavating to build in Colchester still find it.

After Colchester the Iceni went on to London, and very much the same thing happened again. The town was burnt, but this time the Roman people had more warning. Not only did they flee, but they made sure not to leave behind food that would help the Iceni army. This was important. The Iceni must have counted on being able to get food from the stores of their enemies. Without food their huge number of fighters and followers would soon weaken.

But the Iceni went on. The town of St. Albans was also destroyed by fire.

They would not have been able to do this if most of the Roman army had not been far away in North Wales, but things were about to change. Messages reached Wales and the Romans began hurrying south. They were well trained and well organized and they could travel very quickly when they had to.

Boudica's army was much bigger, but quite different. They were not trained fighters, they were angry country people – men, women and children. They could not move quickly because they had brought so many slow wagons with them. They were also weak from hunger.

The last battle of the Iceni was fought in a narrow valley. There was so little space that the Iceni chariots had no room to charge. In front of the Iceni were the Roman soldiers. Behind them were their wagons and families. The narrow valley became a trap. The Iceni were killed or crushed to death, completely overpowered.

Nobody knows what happened to Boudica. Some people think she was killed in the battle. Some believe she escaped, and later drank poison. I believe she died in the battle but I do not know because I was not there.

Someone who was there was a Roman soldier named Agricola. Later Agricola was to become the Roman Governor of Britain.

Kassy was right when she said there were some good Romans. Agricola was a good Roman. Agricola watched the battle from a hilltop and he never forgot what he saw. He told his daughter, Julia, and the man she married, Tacitus.

Tacitus was a Roman historian and he wrote it all down. He wrote a whole book about Agricola. It has been translated into English and I have read it. It tells of the Roman invasion and the suffering of the British people, and Boudica and the Iceni, and it tells us that afterwards things began to change. The Romans began to understand what Kassy and Marcus found out, that it is better to work together than to fight. They began to respect the people whose country they had taken. Agricola was a good Governor. He was fair and brave.

Imagine Agricola and Tacitus talking together, as they so often did. Perhaps Agricola said, "There was an Iceni boy, a brown curly-haired boy with a brown curly-haired dog. They slipped past me together at the end of the day, and I let them go..."

Perhaps that happened. I hope so.

Also available...

I Was There...

Step back
into the fight
for York

VIKING INVASION

My words were drowned as suddenly the world
seemed to be split apart by a huge yell that
roared in the air. The Viking war-cry!

I Was There...

Step back into
the Battle of
Hastings

1066

CLANG! CLANG! CLANG!
The sounds of sword blades crashing against
sword blades, and axes smashing on wooden
shields echoed from the battlefield.

I Was There...

Step back into
the life of a
medieval prince

RICHARD III

We are going to battle! But will I be brave enough to fight like a Prince of the House of York!

I Was There...

Step back into the life of a young actor

SHAKESPEARE'S GLOBE

I don't want to be a farmhand or a butcher.
I want to be a player on the stage at the
Globe playhouse in London!

I Was There...

Step back into
Victorian England

ROYAL NURSEMAID

"I've just heard something amazing." Jane
sounded so excited it made my fingers tingle.
"Queen Victoria is expecting another baby!"

I Was There...

Step back into
the trenches of the
First World War

ALONE IN THE TRENCHES

"*Well, bless my soul. What 'ave we 'ere then?*" *I could make out the shapes of two men. One in a soldier's uniform...*

I Was There...

Step back into
Egypt's Valley
of the Kings

TUTANKHAMUN'S TOMB

Carter ran his hand over the stone.
No one moved. No one spoke. Everyone's
eyes were fixed on him. I held my breath.
Was it the step? Or wasn't it?

You'll be able to imagine
you were really there!